Bowling Over Halloween

This book is fiction. The people, places, events, and fudge mummies depicted within are fictitious. Any resemblance to persons living or dead or to real life places is purely coincidence and, in all honesty, probably a little disturbing.

ISBN 978-0-9728461-9-6

Printed in the U.S.A.

Second Printing, January 2009

Fudge Strikes, Spares Nothing ...

Halloween Goes Down the Gutter!

CONTENTS

Real Heroes Read!

realheroesread.com

#2: Bowling Over Halloween

David Anthony
and
Charles David

Illustrations
Lys Blakeslee

Traverse City, MI

Home of the Heroes

abigail

zoe

andrew

CHAPTER 1:
MEET THE HEROES

Welcome to Traverse City, Michigan, population 18,000. The city has everything you might expect: malls, movie theaters, schools, and playgrounds. Kids swim here in the summer and build snowmen during the winter. Sometimes they pretend that they live in an ordinary place.

But Traverse City is far from ordinary. It is set on one of the Great Lakes and is famous for beautiful fall colors. Thousands of people visit every year.

Still, few of them know the city's real secret. Even fewer talk about it. You see, Traverse City is home to three bold superheroes. This story is about them.

Meet Abigail, the oldest of our heroes by a whole eight minutes. When it comes to sports, she can't be beat—not at baseball, not at bowling, and certainly not at badminton. She can even make more 3-point shots than any pro basketball player. To prove it, she practices hoops by shooting into a sea monster's mouth.

Andrew comes next. He's Abigail's twin brother, younger by a measly eight minutes. If it has wheels, Andrew can ride it. He's a bodacious skater, the bomb on bikes, and totally bad behind the wheel of a racer. Once he even leaped over a swimming pool of hungry sharks while riding a lawn mower. Why? No one knows.

Last but definitely not least is Baby Zoë. She's proof that big things can come in small packages. She still wears a diaper, but she can lift more weight than a bodybuilder. Zoë puts the *awe* in awesome.

Together these three heroes keep the streets and neighborhoods of Traverse City, Michigan, and America safe. Together they are …

CHAPTER 2:
CIDER MILL THRILLS

"Bursting," Baby Zoë groaned, holding her belly.

She was at the cider mill with her whole family. It was Halloween, and they were supposed to be picking out pumpkins. But Zoë had gobbled up too much cider and too many cinnamon donuts. Now she was feeling stuffed. Her super appetite matched her superpowers, not her stomach.

"Batter up," Abigail called out. "It's pumpkin pickin' time."

"Guess who gets to drive the tractor?" Andrew added, smiling as if it were his birthday.

Hearing that got Zoë back on her feet. Andrew was amazing on anything with wheels, but he wasn't always the safest driver. The family might need Zoë's superpowers, and soon.

Thankfully Dad sat up front with Andrew, so the ride was uneventful. Slow and safe, just the way parents liked it. Soon the heroes found themselves in a field so loaded with pumpkins that there were dozens of places to hide.

Abigail found a pumpkin for herself first.

"It's perfect!" she declared, holding it over her head for everyone to see.

Not surprisingly, the pumpkin was shaped like a big football. The sports star had found a pumpkin that fit her athletic personality.

Andrew didn't do too bad himself. His pumpkin was as round and plump as could be. With a little imagination, it would make an ideal fairy tale carriage.

With some special modifications, of course.

Zoë picked the largest pumpkin of all. Without her super-strength, she wouldn't have been able to lift it.

"Big," she grunted, and her parents smiled.

"That's right, Zoë," Mom agreed. "Big indeed. You and your pumpkin are both larger than life."

Little did any of them know that *big* was going to be everybody's problem that Halloween night.

CHAPTER 3:
SUPER-POWERED PUMPKINS

Back home, the heroes tiptoed carefully through the front yard with their pumpkins. Their family went all-out on Halloween, so decorations were everywhere. Tilting tombstones, scraggly scarecrows, grinning ghosts, and a spider's web as big as a hammock crowded the lawn. It was all the heroes could do to keep from bumping into something spooky on the way to the front door.

There were fewer decorations inside, but hardly more room. Zoë's oversized pumpkin took up most of the dining room table.

"Start carving or walk the plank!" Dad exclaimed, slashing the air like a swashbuckler. Dressed like a pirate, he gripped one of those orange-handled carving knives made especially for kids to use on Halloween pumpkins. Not so scary.

"Ugh," Abigail groaned at Dad. "That deserves two minutes in the penalty box. Unless you help us empty out these pumpkins."

Zoë and Andrew agreed. Carving jack-o-lanterns was fun, but cleaning out the guts wasn't.

"Brains," Zoë mumbled, holding up two drippy handfuls of mushy pumpkin innards.

"All righty," Dad said. "I'll show you land-lubbers how it's done. This is how to carve a jack-o-lantern."

For the next twenty minutes, he struggled with his pumpkin. His glasses slid off his nose too many times to count, but he managed to finish without hurting himself.

"Thaaarrrr!" he announced in his pirate accent when he finished. "What do you think, matcys?"

There was nothing wrong with Dad's pumpkin, but it wasn't special either. It was just as average and ordinary as could be. The heroes wanted their pumpkins to stand out, so they decided to use their superpowers.

Abigail carved with a hockey stick, Andrew used a tire iron, and Zoë fired lasers from her eyes.

Seeds popped! Guts oozed! Chunks of pumpkin splattered the room! In half the time Dad had taken, the heroes finished carving. Can you guess which jack-o-lantern belonged to which superhero?

Seeing Zoë frown at her melted pumpkin, Andrew tried to cheer her up. "That's the way to burn
rubber!" he said encouragingly.

Zoë blushed and lowered her eyes. Sometimes
she didn't know her own strength.

"Boo-boo," she mumbled, embarrassed.

CHAPTER 4:
HEROES IN DISGUISE

Now that the pumpkin carving was finished, the heroes hurried to get changed. It was almost time for trick-or-treating, and they didn't want to miss out on a single piece of candy.

Not that they needed to worry about collecting enough candy. A gooey sweet treat was going to be their problem that night.

Abigail was the first one into her costume. Hurrying to get changed was a kind of race, so her athletic super-skills took over. That meant she whipped her siblings, no contest.

The firehouse pole her parents had installed in her room didn't hurt either. It also fit her costume perfectly.

Zoë changed into her costume exactly where you would expect a superhero to change. In an old-fashioned telephone booth. She had one in her room for just such occasions.

When Zoë exited the telephone booth, Andrew tried to give her a scare. He was dressed in his costume already, and thought he looked like a real vampire. Surely he could frighten a baby ladybug!

"I vant to suck your bug," he said in a creepy vampire accent.

Zoë caught her breath and then scowled at Andrew. Shame on him! She knew what the *big* in *big brother* really meant.

It was short for *big mouth*.

"Batty," she said. Then she honked his nose with her thumb and forefinger.

CHAPTER 5:
THE CANDY PLANS CAN

Outside and dressed in their costumes, the heroes discussed trick-or-treating strategies. They each had a plan to get the most candy in the least amount of time. They were *here,* and the candy was *there,* just like a maze on the back of a cereal box.

None of them realized then that Halloween would be canceled. They weren't thinking about anything but bags full of candy.

Abigail snapped her fingers. "Follow me!" she said. "I'll lead us to the goal line. We'll score candy all over Traverse City."

Naturally Andrew thought he had a better plan than his sister did. That, and he couldn't let her be the hero of Halloween.

"Let's get in the wagon instead," he suggested. "I'll pull you guys as fast as I can on my bike. It's got wheels, and I can ride it—to every house in town!"

Wheels and goal lines didn't matter much to Zoë. She had just one thing on her mind, and that was candy.

"Better," she announced, raising one finger into the air like a detective who had solved a riddle. She knew exactly how to get the most candy.

But when Zoë opened her mouth to explain her plan, a massive explosion rocked Halloween night.

CHAPTER 6:
NORTHERN EXPLOSION

"Whoa!" Abigail exclaimed. "Did you hear that? It sounded like an explosion downtown!"

"Let's go check it out!" Andrew cried.

"Bye-bye," Zoë whispered, knowing that trick-or-treating would have to wait. Things were supposed to go bump in the night on Halloween. They weren't supposed to go boom. Traverse City would definitely need its heroes at a time like this.

"Fly up and see where the explosion came from, Zoë," Andrew asked his little sister. "We'll follow you on the ground."

Quick as a rocket, Zoë zipped into the air. Above trees and houses she soared. Over Northwestern Michigan College and the Park Place Hotel she flew. She made the flight in record time, too, and downtown came rapidly into view.

"Bad," Zoë gasped at what she saw there.

    Oh, the horror! Oh, the loss! Zoë couldn't believe her eyes.

    One of Traverse City's yummy fudge shops had exploded. The Pudgie Fudgie was in shambles!

In shock, Zoë stumbled to a landing in front of the Pudgie Fudgie. Andrew and Abigail skidded up next to her a moment later. All three went silent. Their mouths fell open and their eyes bulged.

The shop had exploded, all right. Smoke billowed from its windows. Broken glass sparkled on the ground. There wasn't much left standing except its owner. Thankfully she was still alive, and even appeared unhurt.

Her name was Mrs. Fudgebetter, and she dashed out to meet the heroes. She waved her arms frantically above her head the whole time.

"The fudge is alive!" she wailed. "Help me! Help!"

"What! How?" the twins cried.

Mrs. Fudgebetter shrugged helplessly. "I was baking fudge mummy cookies, and I must have used too much lightning powder in the recipe. My Halloween treats have come to life!"

The danger was worse than the heroes had realized. First the Pudgie Fudgie had exploded. Now the fudge inside had come to life. What a crazy Halloween night, and it was just beginning.

"Don't worry," Abigail told Mrs. Fudgebetter confidently. "We can handle this."

She and her siblings started tiptoeing toward the ruined fudge shop. Who knew what they would discover inside?

CHAPTER 7:
NIGHT OF THE LIVING FUDGE

Before the heroes took three steps, the Pudgie Fudgie started to rumble. Wood creaked and cement cracked.

"Boom?" Zoë wondered, guessing what was about to happen.

"Not again!" Mrs. Fudgebetter howled. She knew what was coming, too. She had seen it before. Her shop was about to explode … again!

Double *boo-oo-oom!*

The second explosion totally flattened the Pudgie Fudgie. It flattened the heroes and Mrs. Fudgebetter, too. When they came to their senses and opened their eyes, they had to look up. *Waaay* up.

A monster the size of a bulldozer towered over them.

Mrs. Fudgebetter shrieked. "My little fudge mummies have grown!"

"Little?" Andrew gawked. There was nothing little about this monster. It was the biggest, blobbiest thing he had ever seen.

Worse, it was moving. With a rumble and a groan, it started to roll. The heroes barely had time to scramble out of its way.

The emergency vehicles that arrived next weren't so lucky.

Glurp! The blob rolled over a fire truck.

Glorp! Gloop! Then over two police cars.

Whum-whum! Down the street it went.

"Bowling!" Zoë cried, and she couldn't have been more right. The fudge blob was bowling over Traverse City. It was bowling over Halloween!

Whatever got in the blob's path was fudged and gobbled up, just like a snowball rolling downhill. Not even Andrew's bike or even poor Mrs. Fudgebetter were safe.

If the heroes didn't find a way to stop the blob, it would bowl over everything in Traverse City.

CHAPTER 8:
BOWLING OVER
TRAVERSE CITY

"Quick!" Andrew shouted. "The blob ate my bike. I need new wheels."

The fudge monster was getting away and taking chunks of Traverse City with it. Only Andrew's superpower would give all three heroes a chance of catching up.

"There!" Abigail pointed. In the middle of the dusty rubble of the Pudgie Fudgie stood a rectangular chest freezer, the kind that opens on the top. It was dented and scratched, but Abigail was right. The freezer did have wheels.

"You're kidding!" Andrew groaned, staring doubtfully at the freezer.

But Abigail smirked at him. "It has wheels, doesn't it?"

And that was that. If it had wheels, Andrew could ride it, even a chest freezer as big as a computer desk. He could ride it, all right, and ride it fast.

"Get on!" he shouted. "It's time to glide on a frozen ride."

"Brrr," Zoë muttered to herself.

Brrr indeed! Andrew got the freezer rolling and hopped on behind his sisters. Chilly October wind blasted them as they rode, but speed was the only way to catch the blob. It was already down the street and heading into the heart of Traverse City.

Of course Andrew loved every second of their ride. He imagined that he and his sisters were surfing the perfect wave on the perfect summer day. Hang thirty, dude!

They chased the blob from one end of Traverse City to the other and back again. Down Front Street and past its cozy shops …

Along the sandy shore of Lake Michigan ...

Around Old Mission Lighthouse …

... And through the movie theater where a spooky Halloween classic was playing on the big screen.

Traverse City had a little bit of everything, and all of what you would want. The question was, where would the blob bowl next?

CHAPTER 9:
MONSTER-MELTING
MEGA-BEAMS

Nothing slowed the fudge monster down. Not bushes, buses, broomsticks, or buffaloes. Yes, buffaloes. Traverse City really did have it all.

Try as he might, Andrew couldn't catch up. He had the freezer moving at top speed, but it just wasn't fast enough. Its little wheels weren't made for high-speed blob chases.

"Zoë, I need your help," Andrew sighed. He hated to admit it, but he and his sisters weren't going to catch the monster this way. They needed to try something else. "Use your laser trick," he said to his baby sister. "Treat that blob like your Halloween pumpkin."

Laser *trick*. *Treat* that blob. Andrew snickered to himself. It was trick or treat, get it?

Off went Zoë, rocketing straight up into the air. Once she was a safe distance above her siblings, she took aim and squinted.

Z-z-z-z-ttt!

Twin lasers the color of molten lava sprang from her eyes. But they weren't simple pumpkin-carving lasers this time. They were monster-melting mega-beams.

"Bzzzt!" Zoë grunted, giving it all she had.

Her lasers burned brighter than ever before, and the night sky blazed with light. Below, Abigail and Andrew threw their arms over their eyes for protection.

When Zoë snapped her eyelids closed, the blaze faded and silence followed for several heartbeats. The heroes almost had time to catch their breath. Then a familiar dreadful sound echoed through the night.

Whum-whum! Whum-whum!

Everyone recognized it immediately. The blob was still bowling and on the move.

The blob was alive! It had survived. Zoë's lasers had barely singed its surface. A little wisp of smoke was the only proof of her attack.

Soon, however, even that disappeared, and so did the blob. It took a sharp right turn and started heading in a deadly new direction.

You see, the monster wasn't satisfied with bowling over just anything anymore. It had been attacked, and now it wanted revenge. It wanted to crush the people responsible. It wanted to crush the heroes.

So the blob changed course and started rolling straight for their neighborhood.

Whum-whum!

CHAPTER 10:
FASTER THAN A SPEEDING BAT

"You've got to warn Mom and Dad!" Abigail told her sister. The blob was headed for their neighborhood, and there wasn't a moment to spare. Andrew's freezer couldn't outrace it. Zoë's lasers couldn't stop it.

"Go, Zoë!" Andrew cried. "Fly as fast as you can!"

Just like that, the race was on. It was Baby Zoë versus the Fudge Monster. Only one of them would win. Only one would be crowned "Faster Than a Speeding Bat" this Halloween.

For the first time that night, something went right. Zoë actually beat the blob. It was a good thing, too, because no one in her neighborhood knew that the monster was coming.

Mom and Dad were cheerfully passing out treats. Kids in costumes scampered from house to house. None of them would have ever guessed that the perfect Halloween was about to be ruined.

Diving like a hawk, Zoë swooped down to her parents. She had only seconds before the blob arrived.

"Beware!" she shouted at the top of her lungs. "Blob!"

Mom glanced at her and smiled. "Where is my sweet little ladybug?" she asked. "Don't make me write you a ticket for being out of costume."

Zoë scowled in frustration. Mom wasn't taking her seriously.

Neither was Dad. He chuckled at Zoë's warning and kept pretending to be a pirate.

"Aye, matey," he drawled. "That story sounds
like a tale for our next camping trip. Beware of the
blob on Halloween!"

He laughed in a spooky voice after he said it.
Mwa-ha-ha-hah!

That was all the time Zoë got. One warning and two chances. Mom and Dad didn't believe her, and now it was too late.

Whoo-oom!

The blob arrived like a herd of charging elephants. It smashed through the neighbors' house. It bowled over the neighbors' car. And the closer it came to Zoë, the faster it rolled.

"Bigger!" Zoë gasped.

Not only was the blob rolling faster, but it had grown, too. Now it was the size of a tyrannosaurus rex. Whatever got stuck in it made it that much bigger, and there was a lot of Traverse City stuck in it already. Soon it would be as big as an asteroid!

Zoë had time to do just one thing. Save her parents or try again to stop the monster. It was a tough choice, but sometimes that was what being a hero was all about.

She paused a moment to think and then snatched Mom and Dad by their collars and prepared to take off into the air. Nothing was more important than her parents.

Behind them, the blob loomed like a black hole against the night sky. It was coming to swallow them whole.

CHAPTER 11:
FREEZER MEETS FUDGE

"Blob!" Mom shrieked.

"Beware!" Dad howled.

Now they believed Zoë. Now that they saw the blob. They believed and screamed, but it was too late to run. Zoë had them by the collar, and the blob had them in its sights.

Before Zoë could get her parents safely into the air, the blob struck. Splack! It bowled over the three of them like a sticky steamroller.

Down they went, smothered in fudge. How tasty—if they weren't being flattened. Then up, up, and over they went, rolling with the blob. Like the neighbors' car, they were stuck in the fudge. The blob really had swallowed them whole!

Just then Abigail and Andrew arrived. They were still riding the freezer, and Andrew had its wheels smoking.

"The blob has Mom and Dad!" Abigail cried. "And Zoë, too!"

Hearing that, Andrew made a fast and dangerous decision. He couldn't allow the blob to escape again, and he could think of only one way to stop it.

"Brace yourself," he said fiercely. "We're going to ram it."

What happened next was loud, messy, dangerous, and just crazy enough to work. Andrew set a
collision course for the blob and let the freezer do
the rest. He didn't turn. He didn't slow. He just told
his sister when to jump.

"Now!" he bellowed as they approached the
monster. Then he and Abigail leaped over the side
of the speeding freezer.

SPLOO-OO-OOM!

When the freezer met the fudge, things got sticky. Chocolate chunks hurtled here and there. Peanut butter bits spattered the ground like hail.

All Andrew and Abigail could do was hit the dirt, throw their arms over their heads, and hope for the best. Except for a mess, neither of them knew what to expect when the blob exploded.

What they definitely didn't expect was Zoë. But in the middle of the explosion, one object splattered louder when it landed than the others. In fact, it splattered twice and was followed by a groan.

"*B*-bouncing," Zoë grunted.

The twins looked up to see their baby sister lying on the hood of a car. She was covered in fudge but unhurt. The same could not be said for the car.

"Get up, Zoë!" Abigail exclaimed.

Andrew looked around at the gooey mess. There was no blob in sight.

"We won!" he cheered. "We beat the fudge monster and saved Halloween."

But Zoë shook her head and pointed a pudgy hand forward. "Bouncing," she repeated firmly.

And then the twins saw what she saw. The blob wasn't beaten and Halloween hadn't been saved. The monster was bouncing down the street like a giant soccer ball, crushing everything in its path.

CHAPTER 12:
BULLYING THE BULLY

As a group, the heroes had never felt more like losers. The blob had destroyed their neighborhood, fudge-napped their parents, and escaped.

Worse, it was more powerful and destructive than ever. Instead of simply rolling, the blob was bouncing now. Ramming it with the freezer had caused that to happen.

"Bully!" Zoë snarled, shaking a tiny fist at the monster as it bounced into the distance.

Abigail snapped her fingers. "That's it, Zoë!" she exclaimed. "You're a genius!"

And with that, she tore off down the street after the blob. Her athletic power kicked in immediately, and her legs became a blur. What superhuman speed!

All Zoë and Andrew could do was root their sister on. They couldn't match her speed, and they couldn't stop her. So they cheered and clapped and hoped she knew what she was doing.

At the end of the block, Abigail caught the blob. There she stopped, put her hands on her hips, and shouted after the monster.

"Fudge isn't so great!" she said. "You're just a benchwarmer, not an all-star. You'll never be in the starting line-up."

Everyone up and down the street heard Abigail shout. Andrew and Zoë heard her. The trick-or-treaters heard her. The blob heard her. Everyone heard and then they froze.

What was she trying to do, make the blob madder? It was already destroying Traverse City. Angering it would only make things worse.

But Abigail wasn't finished yet. She shouted again.

"I would rather do homework all weekend than eat fudge!"

When the blob heard Abigail's second insult, it didn't stay frozen. It got mad and wanted to crush her. No one was supposed to like homework more than fudge!

So with a mighty whoomp, it threw itself against a nearby house like a basketball against a backboard. The force of the collision sent it bouncing in the opposite direction. Back up the street toward Abigail.

She screamed. The monster was coming for her.

CHAPTER 13:
MORE FUN THAN FUDGE

Whoomp! Whoomp!

The blob thundered after Abigail like a boulder crashing downhill. Every bounce propelled it closer. Every thump shook the ground.

Soon its tremors became too much. Abigail stumbled and went down, her arms and legs sprawling. There she panted, trying to catch her breath. She couldn't run any farther, and the blob was almost on top of her.

Andrew arrived on his skateboard. He hadn't just been waiting around. He had found a way to follow his sister.

So now he did the running for her, but he didn't use his feet. He used his mouth. Running it wasn't a superpower, but he was still an expert. His teachers often accused him of running his mouth in class.

"Over here, fudge-face!" he shouted at the blob. "Don't listen to her. I would rather clean my room than eat fudge. What do you think of that?" He jumped up and down, too, and waved his arms wildly so that the blob would spot him.

Not a second passed before the monster re-acted. It rotated toward Andrew like a searchlight and groaned from somewhere deep inside. Then it started rolling toward him with unexpected speed.

"That's right!" Andrew continued. "Cleaning up is more fun than fudge. My dirty socks rock!"

Of course Andrew didn't believe a single word he was saying. Neither did Abigail. She didn't like homework. He didn't like cleaning. And neither of them really thought that dirty socks rocked. Especially not Andrew's. *Pee-yew!*

What the twins were really doing was taking Zoë's advice. They were bullying the bully. They were pretending to dislike fudge so that the blob would get angry with them.

And it was working, too. Instead of randomly destroying Traverse City, the blob was chasing the heroes. If they could keep the monster mad enough for long enough, maybe they could save Halloween.

The question now was, where should they go? Sure, the blob was chasing them, but they couldn't just run in circles. They had to go somewhere, and nowhere seemed safe.

Jail was their first thought, but it wouldn't work. The monster would never fit inside and would just ooze through the bars anyway. And tricking it into Lake Michigan would probably turn it into some kind of Fudge Ness Monster. The Great Lakes would never be safe again!

Where, then, should the heroes lead the blob?

CHAPTER 14:
MACKINAC GEMINI JUMP

"Which way?" Andrew gasped, arms pumping and skating hard. The blob was after him now instead of Abigail, and he had no idea where to go. He only knew that he had to go fast.

"Baseball!" Zoë answered, not that Andrew understood why. Playing with the blob wasn't going to help. He doubted it could even hit Abigail's major league curve ball.

Abigail, however, understood immediately. Maybe it took a sports expert to figure it out so quickly. Zoë didn't want to play with the blob. She wanted to trap it, and a baseball field was just the right size.

"Are you thinking where I'm thinking?" Abigail asked her sister.

Zoë beamed, thrilled at being understood. "Beach Bums!" she cheered.

The Beach Bums was Traverse City's professional baseball team. Abigail went to almost all of the games, which were played at Wuerfel Park. Best of all, the field had walls and fences surrounding it on all sides. If the heroes could coax the blob into it, they could trap it there. Then they could figure out how to defeat the monster without endangering more of Traverse City and its citizens.

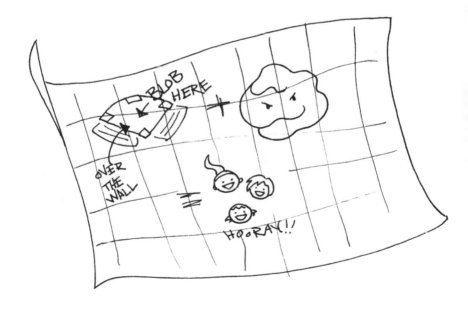

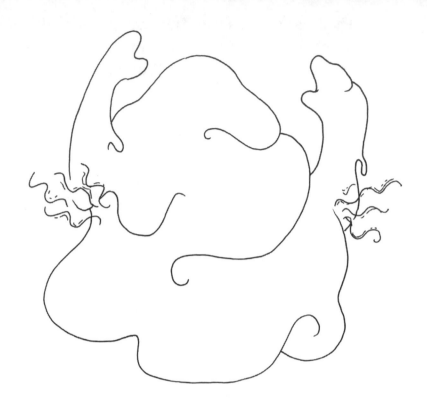

They reached the park barely ahead of the blob. Andrew and Abigail kept it angry and chasing them by hurling insults over their shoulders. In the commotion, it didn't notice Zoë slip away.

"Sludge and fudge rhyme for a reason!" Andrew shouted. "So do slob and blob!"

"You should run over a telephone pole," Abigail suggested. "You could be a shish-ka-blob."

"Some people have body odor. You have *blobby* odor!"

Meanwhile, Zoë set their trap. She flew north and east to where Michigan's upper and lower peninsulas met. There stood the mighty Mackinac Bridge. It was 26,372 feet long. That's over five miles!

Thankfully Zoë didn't need that much bridge. She needed only a piece. So she paid the toll, grabbed a section as long as the average driveway, and sped back to Traverse City. As she flew away, she promised to return the piece as soon as possible.

"Borrow!" she explained.

She returned to the baseball park seconds before her siblings ran out of room. The blob was closing in behind them. The stadium fence loomed directly ahead.

"Put it down, Zoë," said Abigail. Sure, she could outrace the blob and anyone else, but she needed room to run.

"But don't make it too steep!" Andrew added. He knew what was coming and wanted to be sure they could get airborne.

Zoë worried about that, too. So when she set down her piece of the bridge, she did it at just the right angle. One end went in the stadium's parking lot. The other rested on the outfield fence. What she was left with was a ramp big enough for the blob.

"Up we go!" Abigail shouted, jumping suddenly into Andrew's arms like Scooby-Doo into Shaggy's. But she wasn't afraid, she was getting ready to perform a daring skateboarding trick with her brother.

"Hang on!" Andrew cried. "Here goes the first ever Mackinac Gemini Jump!"

Then together they hit the ramp and rocketed into the air.

Abigail and Andrew were flying. They were in the air and free. Finally they understood why Zoë rarely walked. Why walk when she could fly?

But unlike their sister, the twins couldn't stay in the air for long. Already they were falling, and the ground was racing nearer. In seconds they were going to crash into the baseball field's dugout.

CHAPTER 15:
FUDGE IN THE OUTFIELD

"Andrew, do something!" Abigail howled at her brother. "We're going to crash!"

She wasn't kidding either. The dugout was directly below them, and they were running out of air. Andrew's skateboard needed wings if he expected it to save them.

"Relax," he replied. "I've got mad skills. We'll be safe."

"You're mad, all right," Abigail snapped. "Mad like a scientist."

As much as Abigail liked adventure, she wasn't going to leave their landing to chance or Andrew. The dugout was made mostly of concrete, and hitting it would hurt. So she rummaged quickly through her duffel bag, hoping against hope.

"Please, please, please," she repeated. Then, "Aha!" Out came her umpire's chest protector. It wasn't exactly a piece of sports equipment like a ball or puck, but what else would you call it?

"Quick, sit on this," she told Andrew.

A moment later, the chest protector hit the top of the dugout and bounced. Bloing! Andrew and Abigail went with it.

Back into the air they flew. Only this time they weren't on a skateboard and their flight wasn't planned. They were flying out of control.

"Well?" Andrew asked, clutching the chest protector with white knuckles.

But before Abigail could respond, Zoë snatched the chest protector from below. Then up they sped, leaving the dugout and baseball field far below.

"Bozos," Zoë teased. What would the twins do without her?

Once the heroes reached a safe height, Zoë stopped ascending. Then the three gazed down upon Wuerfel Park and its chocolaty captive.

Exactly as they had hoped, the blob had tried to follow them. It had rolled up the ramp and then hurtled into the ballpark. Now it was trapped! The blob couldn't roll over the stadium's seats or the outfield fence, and it didn't have a super-powered baby sister or chest protector to help it escape.

"Looks like we bowled the last strike," Abigail smirked.

Her siblings had to agree. The blob was huge and gooey, but they had outsmarted it. Now all they had to do was free the people who were stuck inside it and then shrink it down to less-than-monster size.

"Bombdrops," Zoë suggested, and the twins cheered. They were finally going to get to go trick-or-treating. Doing so would save Halloween.

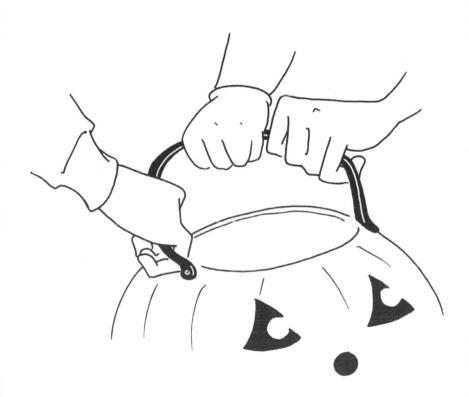

CHAPTER 16:
TRICK-OR-TREAT

Bombdrops were exactly what the heroes needed. They were gumdrop-shaped candy with an explosive surprise. Chew a piece, blow a bubble, pop it, and BOOM! Candy didn't get louder or more fun.

Best of all, the heroes knew right where to find some. A lady in their neighborhood named Diana Might passed out bombdrops every year. Trick-or-treating at her house would save the day, and Halloween.

But first they needed their costumes. So the heroes raced home, got changed, and then zoomed to Mrs. Might's house. Luckily the blob hadn't rolled down her street.

"Trick-or-treat!" Andrew and Abigail called. Almost immediately, the front door burst open. Everything about Mrs. Might was loud—her candy, her house, and her voice.

"HAPPY HALLOWEEN, CHILDREN!" she bellowed in greeting. "I HOPE YOU'RE HAVING A BLAST!" Chewing explosive candy had taught her to appreciate the noisy things in life.

Plip! Plap! Plup! Into their sacks she plopped one bombdrop each. Enough for fun and fireworks, but not enough to take care of the blob.

After she closed the door, Andrew sighed. "Three pieces isn't going to be enough," he said. "We need more."

Zoë thought for a minute and then removed the ladybug antennas from her head. Then she handed them to Andrew.

"Bluff?" she asked with a wink.

"That's it!" Abigail exclaimed. "Homerun! We'll swap costumes and try again."

Minutes later they were dressed in each other's costumes and back on Mrs. Might's front porch. "Trick-or-treat!" Abigail and Andrew called again.

This time when the door burst open, Mrs. Might was louder than ever.

"YOU NEED TO DO BETTER THAN THAT," she boomed. "I RECOGNIZE THOSE COSTUMES. IF YOU WANT MORE CANDY, BLOW ME AWAY WITH A TRICK."

Thinking fast, Zoë scooped up the pumpkins on the porch and started to juggle.

Mrs. Might's mouth fell open, and for once her voice was a whisper. As quiet as a mouse just wasn't her normal volume.

"You're the bomb!" she gasped at Zoë. "Here, take the whole bowl. A trick like that deserves it."

Then she dumped all of her bombdrops into Zoë's bag. Tiny explosions burst in the sack as the candies collided, but Zoë held on and ignored them. She and her siblings finally had enough firepower to send the blob to the moon.

CHAPTER 17:
OPERATION: BOMBDROP

Back at the ballpark, Andrew was the first to give the bombdrops a try. He hit the outfield fence on his skateboard and started to grind his way around the field. As he went, he tossed handfuls of candy at the blob.

"Here's a new trick," he boasted. "The Grand Slam Grind. It's baseball and skateboarding put together. Tony Hawk will love it!"

Zoë patrolled the air. As quickly as she could chew and blow bubbles, she dropped inflated candies onto the monster like water balloons from a balcony.

"Bombardier!" she squealed, taking aim. She felt as if she were in a real-life video game. High score for the hero!

Last but not least came Abigail. A baseball field was her home away from home, so it was her job to bat clean-up in Operation: Bombdrop.

At a full sprint, she rounded third base and headed for home. The blob waited for her there like a catcher blocking the plate. But this was the Halloween World Series, and Abigail would not be denied.

She hit the dirt in a slide and heaved the bag of bombdrops at the blob. Then—glomp!—a mouth appeared in the blob that swallowed the bag whole.

Triple *boo-oo-oom!*

For the third time that Halloween, a huge explosion rocked and rattled Traverse City. The heroes were thrown backward, and the blob burst from the inside out. Eating too much candy really could give you a belly ache!

When the fudge settled, the blob was gone. Hunks of chocolate, assorted nuts, and fudge mummy cookies littered the ball field.

There were people, too, covered in fudge and holding their heads. They had just been spun round and round in the world's fudgiest Ferris wheel. Most were kids in costumes. Some were parents and adults from around town. One was Mrs. Fudgebetter.

"My poor fudge mummies!" she sobbed. "This wasn't supposed to happen."

"There, there," Andrew said, patting Mrs. Fudgebetter on the shoulder. "You can make more cookies. Don't worry."

Zoë nodded and smiled. "Bake," she agreed.

To the heroes, the danger and bad times were over. The blob was no more, and the townsfolk were free. Traverse City had been saved.

So then why was Mrs. Fudgebetter still so upset?

It didn't take long for them to find out. With a snarl, Mrs. Fudgebetter leaped to her feet.

"Back off!" she snapped at the heroes. "You've almost ruined everything."

From her apron she pulled her canister of lightning powder. That was the stuff that had caused the blob to come to life. Then she started to shake it wildly as if trying to salt the biggest bowl of popcorn ever popped.

"Rise, my fudge mummies!" she shrieked. "Rise and attack!"

Wherever the lightning powder landed, fudge mummy cookies twitched and sat up straight. They were coming to life like the Frankenstein monster.

CHAPTER 18:
WHEN FUDGE ATTACKS

Mrs. Fudgebetter wasn't at all who the heroes thought she was. She wasn't a sweet storeowner and brilliant baker. She was a madwoman who wanted to destroy Traverse City!

In the backroom of her Pudgie Fudgie fudge shop, she had cooked up a recipe for disaster. She had baked a batch of monsters.

And now they were attacking.

Fudge mummy cookies staggered toward the heroes from every direction. Instead of one blob, the heroes were facing an army.

It was three against three hundred, more than impossible. Even superheroes had their limits.

"Stay together," Abigail growled.

"Bravery," added Zoë.

Words and courage were all they had left. They couldn't hope to win against such odds. Finding a unicorn with a winning lottery ticket in its mouth was more likely.

Still they fought and gave it their best. That was what made them heroes. They did what was right no matter how hard or impossible it seemed.

Andrew attacked, Zoë zapped, and Abigail didn't hold back. They did what they could, but it wasn't enough. Soon the fudge mummies dragged them to the ground. There were just too many of them.

It should have been over. Mrs. Fudgebetter should have won. But an amazing rescue came from somewhere the heroes least expected.

"It's trick-or-treating time!" one of the towns-folk shouted, and a cheer swept through the people of Traverse City. In a surprise rush, they dashed forward and started stuffing fudge mummy cookies into their mouths.

Everyone who had been stuck in the blob was eating a cookie or three. Students from Silver Lake and Cherry Knoll munched. Horizon Books' customers crunched.

Best of all, the fudge mummies didn't mind. Cookies were made to be eaten, after all. Even Mrs. Fudgebetter realized that now.

So while the heroes and townsfolk were busy chewing, she tucked her lightning power under her arm and quietly crept away into the night.

CHAPTER 19:
THE DAY AFTER
HALLOWEEN

A short time later, Abigail, Andrew, and the rest of the townsfolk were stuffed. Never before had they felt so full. And on Halloween, that said a lot.

Only Zoë hadn't eaten too much. She remembered what had happened at the cider mill earlier, and she had important things still to do.

"Beautify," she said, taking off into the sky.

For the next hour, Zoë worked around town. She reset mailboxes, raised fallen buildings, and righted overturned cars. She repaired, rebuilt, and remodeled. She even returned her piece of the Mackinac Bridge. When she finished, Traverse City looked almost as good as new. Her timing was perfect, too, because the townsfolk were finally starting to feel better.

"No more Pudgie Fudgie fudge for me," Mom groaned.

The heroes agreed. They didn't want to think about fudge any more that day. Only their beds were on their minds. They had had a long day and an even longer night.

"Bedtime?" Zoë asked behind a yawn.

The parents thought that was a great idea. It was time for bed. But the kids in their costumes complained.

"What about Halloween?" they asked. "What about the *candy?*"

To make everyone happy, trick-or-treating was rescheduled for the next evening. Once again the kids of Traverse City put on their costumes and filled the streets and sidewalks. There were all kinds of candy and treats to be had, and not a single piece bowled over anything in town.

Halloween had finally been saved.

Nevertheless, the heroes kept a watchful eye out for danger. They knew it could strike at anytime, anywhere. Holidays weren't necessarily safe. Neither were normal days. In fact, next summer they would be challenged again, this time by …

Book #3:
Cherry Bomb Squad

realheroesread.com

Real Heroes Read!

#1: Alien Ice Cream
#2: Bowling Over Halloween
#3: Cherry Bomb Squad
#4: Digging For Dinos
#5: Easter Egg Haunt
#6: Fowl Mouthwash

... and more!

**Visit
www.realheroesread.com
for the latest news**

Want to Order Your Very Own Autographed
Heroes A2Z or Knightscares Book?

Here's How:

(1) Check the books you want on the next page.
(2) Fill out the address information at the bottom.
(3) Add up the total price for the books you want.

Heroes A2Z cost $4.99 each.
Knightscares cost $5.99 each.

(4) Add $1.00 shipping per book.
(5) Michigan residents include 6% sales tax.
(6) Send check or money order along with the next page to:

Real Heroes Read!
P.O. Box 654
Union Lake, MI 48387

Thank You!

Please allow 3-4 weeks for shipping

☐ Heroes A2Z #1: Alien Ice Cream

☐ Heroes A2Z #2: Bowling Over Halloween

☐ Heroes A2Z #3: Cherry Bomb Squad

☐ Heroes A2Z #4: Digging For Dinos

☐ Heroes A2Z #5: Easter Egg Haunt

☐ Heroes A2Z #6: Fowl Mouthwash

☐ Knightscares #1: Cauldron Cooker's Night

☐ Knightscares #2: Skull in the Birdcage

☐ Knightscares #3: Early Winter's Orb

☐ Knightscares #4: Voyage to Silvermight

☐ Knightscares #5: Trek Through Tangleroot

☐ Knightscares #6: Hunt for Hollowdeep

☐ Knightscares #7: The Ninespire Experiment

☐ Knightscares #8: Aware of the Wolf

Total $ Enclosed: _____

Autograph To: _____

Name: _____

Address: _____

City, State, Zip: _____

Abigail.
When it comes to
sports,
she can't be beat.

Andrew.
If it has wheels,
he can ride it.

Baby Zoë.
Superhero in a diaper.

Also by David Anthony and Charles David

Monsters. Magic. Mystery.

#1: Cauldron Cooker's Night
#2: Skull in the Birdcage
#3: Early Winter's Orb
#4: Voyage to Silvermight
#5: Trek Through Tangleroot
#6: Hunt for Hollowdeep
#7: The Ninespire Experiment
#8: Aware of the Wolf

**Visit
www.realheroesread.com
to learn more**

#1: Cauldron Cooker's Night

#2: Skull in the Birdcage

#3: Early Winter's Orb

#4: Voyage to Silvermight
The Dragonsbane Horn Book One

#5: Trek Through Tanglewood
The Dragonsbane Horn Book Two

#6: Hunt in Hollowdeep
The Dragonsbane Horn Book Three

#7: The Vinespire Experiment

#8: Aware of the Wolf

About the Illustrator
Lys Blakeslee

Lys graduated from Grand Valley State University in Michigan where she earned a degree in Illustration.

She has always loved to read, and devoted much of her childhood to devouring piles of books from the library.

She lives in Wyoming, MI with her wonderful parents, two goofy cats, and one extra-loud parakeet.

Broccoli, spinach, and ice cream are a few of her favorite foods.

Thank you, Lys!